For Kate and Jane, my two favorite chicks —D.M.

For my favorite fuzzy creatures, Cash and Pico —S.H.

IMPRINT
A part of Macmillan Publishing Group, LLC
120 Broadway, New York, NY 10271

ABOUT THIS BOOK
The art in this book was created with pencils and watercolor and completed digitally.
The text was set in Adobe Caslon, and the display type is Gumley.
The book was edited by Erin Stein and designed by Natalie C. Sousa.
The production was supervised by Raymond Ernesto Colón, and the production editor was Dawn Ryan.

FIVE FUZZY CHICKS. Text copyright © 2020 by Diana Murray. Illustrations copyright © 2020 by Imprint.
All rights reserved. Printed in China by RR Donnelley Asia Printing
Solutions Ltd., Dongguan City, Guangdong Province.

Library of Congress Cataloging-in-Publication Data is available.

ISBN 978-1-250-30122-2 (hardcover)

Our books may be purchased in bulk for promotional, educational, or business use. Please contact your local bookseller or the
Macmillan Corporate and Premium Sales Department at (800) 221-7945 ext. 5442
or by email at MacmillanSpecialMarkets@macmillan.com.

Imprint logo designed by Amanda Spielman

First edition, 2020

10 9 8 7 6 5 4 3 2 1

mackids.com

Steal this book and fear the worst
for you will soon be gravely cursed.
You'll grow a beak and never talk,
but flap your wings, and cluck, and squawk.
You'll scratch and peck the ground all day
and spend your nights in scratchy hay.
If turning chicken has you scared,
heed this warning to be spared.

Five Fuzzy Chicks

written by Diana Murray   illustrated by Sydney Hanson

{Imprint}
MAKE YOUR MARK
New York

Out on the farm,
it's been a long day.
Sun's setting low.
Night's on the way.

Everyone's tired.
All the work's done.
But five fuzzy chicks . . .

want to run, run, run, run!

Five fuzzy chicks
run past the plow,
into the grass,
and under the cow.

The cow says, "Moo! Moo!"
The chicks say, "Cheep! Cheep!"

But the grass is so cozy . . .

one chick falls asleep.

Four fuzzy chicks
skip by the pigs,
hop on a rock,
and dance silly jigs.

The pigs say, "Oink! Oink!"
The chicks say, "Cheep! Cheep!"

But the moss is so soft . . .

one chick falls asleep.

Three fuzzy chicks
dance in the clover,
hop past the fence,
and right over Rover!

The dog says, "Woof! Woof!"
The chicks say, "Cheep! Cheep!"

But the dog is so snuggly . . .

one chick falls asleep.

Two fuzzy chicks,
skipping along,
pass by the horse
and sing him a song.

The horse says, "Neigh! Neigh!"
The chicks sing, "Cheep! Cheep!"

But the hay is so comfy . . .

one chick falls asleep.

One fuzzy chick
out to have fun
hops by the sheep . . .
and counts every one.

The sheep say, "Baa! Baa!"
The chick *starts* to cheep,

but before she can finish . . .

she falls fast asleep.

Chicks sleeping here.
Chicks sleeping there.
In the grass, by the stable!
Chicks everywhere!

Mama Hen hurries
to gather her troop.
She scoops them all up . . .

. . . and runs back to the coop.

She whispers, "Cluck, cluck."
The chicks whisper, "Cheep."

And their nest is so quiet . . .
five chicks fall asleep.